Caliban's Redemption

Poetry in Process

By

David William Parry

Copyright © David Parry and Mandrake of Oxford, 03
First edition

All rights reserved. No part of this work may be reproduced or utilized in any form by any means electronic or mechanical, including *xerography, photocopying, microfilm,* and *recording,* or by any information storage system without permission in writing from the author.

Published by
Mandrake of Oxford
PO Box 250
OXFORD
OX1 1AP (UK)

A CIP catalogue record for this book is available from the British Library and the US Library of Congress.

ISBN 1 869928 75X

Contents

Acknowledgements 4
Midnight's Monk 5
Our Sweetgrass Supper 53
The Fool and His Fathers 92

Acknowledgements

I would like to thank all of those who have helped to make this book manifest, in particular Mr Richard Rudgley, Dr. Bernard Hoose, Dr. Brian Clack and the late Mr Christopher Johnson who taught me to fully appreciate the dark light of critical analysis.

Also I would like to thank the innumerable students of literature who have discussed the material with me. I am especially grateful to Mr Simon J. Powley, who in addition to typing this manuscript, has been a continual source of support with his diligent reading of the text and numerous helpful suggestions.

Lastly, it is my privilege to dedicate this book to Konrad K Szalapski, whose redemptive heart allowed Caliban to feel a love which illumines the sun and all the stars.

Midnight's Monk

Caliban, the dark but not damned, who was a shadow within his own twilight, had waited eleven years in the town of Faram for his caravan that was to return and bear him back to the primeval forests of his birth.

And in the eleventh year, on the thirty-first evening of October, the month of spirits, he climbed the high hill outside the town walls and looked towards the icy distance; and he saw his caravan arriving with the night.

Yet as he descended the hill, a vengeance came upon him and he thought in his spleen: how can I go in silence from my prison? Not without a moment's thunder can my anger leave this place. Long were the nights of solitude that I have spent in its streets and longer still were the days of bitter poverty. Am I so weak as to depart from my poison without a single incantation?

No! Far too many fragments of my heart have been scattered in these unfeeling streets and endless seem the children of my desire that walk in destitution amongst those hills. Therefore, I cannot withdraw from Faram without the sensation of blood and fire.

It is not a past that I cast away this evening, but a failure that I tear with the strength of my own hands. Nor is it a memory that I leave behind me, but a nightmare made sour with thirst and hunger.

But I cannot wait much longer.

The blood that calls its people back to a secret homeland also calls to me, and I must depart.

Spirited away. For to stay as the hours pale into the day is to forgive in weakness and dissolve into a shapeless torpor. Rather would I leave all that is here and regain my shape. But how shall I?

My screams cannot remove the pain of experience that gave them birth. Unaided must they seek expression.

Truth alone, and without exception, shall bring my solitude into the form of survival.

And truth is my greatest weapon.

Now, when Caliban reached the foot of the hill he turned towards the dazzling night and he saw his caravan approaching the outer limits of the town, and upon their huge horses the gigantic men of his own land.

And his heart cried out to them, and he whispered:

Sons of my sacred father, you who ride the winds of an ancient destiny, how often have you ridden into my desires? And now you come with the nocturnal dreams of a deeper awakening.

Too long have I been ready to leave, and my eagerness breaks into a gallop.

Only another star is needed in the sky to set me free, only another demon in his infernal place. And then I shall stand with you as a man amongst magicians.

Then the road that leads towards my home will become a living vehicle revealing the quickest way to Hell.

Only another moment will this moon take. Only another minute to reach her space.

And then I shall return to you, a prodigal son at last forgiven.

However, as he walked he saw afar both men and women leaving their houses and their pleasures and hastening towards the town centre.

And he heard their voices murmuring his name from tavern to

tower and telling one another of the coming of his caravan.

And he sneered to himself: shall the night of tempest also be the night of sovereignty?

And shall it be said that parting was in truth my power?

What indeed shall I say to him who has left his brothel with an unfulfilled delight or to him who has left a glass of fresh and frothy ale?

Should my bowels become a bakery from which wafers of excrement are served as a Eucharistic meal to the fool and his senile fathers?

And shall my urine flow like a fountain of wine that I may ever fill their unsuspecting chalice?

Am I a drum that the hand of mighty powers may play to make men march into war and woe, or a pipe that will call these people into pain?

A seeker of subtleties am I, and the power I have found in their pursuit I will not cast before an ignorant herd.

If this is my night of saving, then the seeds I spread shall be an everlasting curse, and my personal darkness will be the light to nurture tares in a season of dreadful storms.

If this is indeed the moment in which I lift up my torch, it is not my secret that shall burn therein.

Firm and furious shall I raise my wand, and the bright spirit of the Northern star shall enter into it with prophecies and vision.

These things he said in silence. But much in his stomach boiled with the need for self-expression. For he himself had a hankering to put his fury into raging words.

When he entered the courtyard of the town all the people came to greet him, and they were weeping with the fears of death and execution.

And the elders of the town stood forth and said with one voice:

Go quickly and in peace.

An eclipse have you been in the summer of our dreams and your leaving has given us hopes to hope.

A stranger you remain amongst us, and an unwanted guest, whose presence is to us blind terror.

Let our eyes no longer see you and our ears no longer hear your magic.

Let the distance of our countries now separate us for ever, and the time you have spent with us fade in nature's memory.

You have walked among us a dwarf with words of cyclopean fire which scorched our faces and your bile has blistered our frail bodies.

Much have we despised you. But speak to us of abomination that all sides may learn to forget. Even now we would be ignorant and stand with disregard before you.

As ever has it been that banishment knows not its own depth until the hour of departure.

And others came also and begged for peace. Yet Caliban answered them not. He only bent his head and smiled; and those who stood near him saw the glint of razor sharp teeth.

And he and the people proceeded towards the entrance of the great square and its church. And there came out of the presbytery an old man whose name was Meekan. And he was a priest.

And Meekan looked upon the dwarf with loathing for it was he who had first heard of his magic and feared him when he had been but an evening in their town.

And Meekan hailed him, saying:

Prophet of the benighted, in quest of the forbidden, long have you spied the distances for your caravan.

And now your caravan of cadavers has come to us, and you must needs go away.

Deep is your longing for the land of your demons and the dwelling place of your greatest devils; but our fear would not bind you, nor our blindness hold you. However, this we ask of you before you leave us, that you speak to us and give us your blessing.

And we will tell our children that they are safe in their beds, and they will in turn tell their children not to fear the night.

In your aloneness you have prowled our nights and in your endarkenment you have overheard the weeping and lamentations of our sleep.

Now therefore leave us in peace to ourselves and tell us nothing of your wisdom which hìdes a blade in its skull.

And Caliban answered:

People of Faram, of what can I speak save that which you shun in your own souls?

Then said Meekan, speak to us of hate and the venomous limits of its dominion. Tell us how to avoid its evil.

And Caliban raised his head in authority, and fixed the people with the force of his stare, and there fell a stillness upon them as in a shock of imminent danger.

And with a voice like sulphur he said:

When hate follows you, embrace him, though his ways are hard to fathom.

And when his vampire wings enfold you, learn to yield your unprotected veins.

Although the teeth he bears may bite you.

Then your voice will speak with the power of his tongue and shatter the boundaries of his endless promises as the gale sweeps upon a sacred wasteland.

For even as hate fells you, so shall he empower you. Even as he is a hunger, so is he a chance to feed. Even as he descends to your essence and promises your body enough strength to fly, so shall he ascend in arrogance to your brow and cloak sweating muscles with their victory.

Like a lover he gathers you to his chest.

He wrestles with you in his nakedness.

He holds you to the floor with ease.

He bleeds you to a whiteness.

He kills you to a former life.

And then he raises you to a spiritual perfection where death itself has finally been overcome.

All these things shall hate to do to transform you from an eternal victim into an immortal hunter with the rest of the time as your personal prey.

But if in your fear you would seek only escape from the protection of hate and hate's kingdom, then it is better for you to end your pallid life in suicide than prolong the bitter and empty years ahead.

Entering into a world of anaemic shades where no-one can laugh, or sing, nor weep the tears of a tragic beauty.

Hate gives itself unreservedly and takes nothing except the weakness of a child.

For hate is the virility of the strong.

When you hate you should not say 'I have the strength of a giant', but rather 'I am a giant amongst the strong'.

And think not that hate will overwhelm your mind, for hate, if he finds you worthy, will grant you the cunning of a million years.

Hate has no other desire than to succeed.

But if you hate and succeed in your hatred, let the eloquence of success then proceed to extreme actions.

To melt the face of a sinless baby and use its running fat as an offering towards the infinite night.

To know the rhapsody of a rapist.

To wound and to kill the saints and patrons who aid you in ill-health.

And to bleed willingly in the fight.

To wake at dusk with the voice of a thousand screeching demons and to give thanks for another deadly evening.

To rest as a monk at midnight in murderous meditation of hate's ecstasy.

To return home at dawn in exhausted satisfaction.

And then to sleep with a litany of praises to the power in your arms and the purpose of your spirit.

*

I laid a black lotus
Upon the endarkened alter of Setibos
In order to bind your heart
To mine

*

i
ii
i
ii
i
ii
i
i

Miranda

I love you holy virgin,
with the soul that you have moulded,
lovely as a rosebud,
to the silver moon unfolded.
I love you holy virgin.

I love you Queen of Heaven,
with the body you have fashioned,
twisted in your service,
by sacred sighs of divine passion.
I love you Queen of Heaven.

I love you aged mother,
with the mind that you have hardened,
deep as dark obsidian,
reflecting black thoughts yet unpardoned.
I love you aged mother.

I love you,
I praise you,
I abase myself before you,
and with golden songs adore you,
my holy whore of heaven.

*

The violence
In our ambitions
Is always a sign
Of similar spirits.

*

*

Even demons
Benighting the deepest hell
Still need to believe
In love.

*

*

Your tender cup
Of youthful longing
Thrills to the salted taste
Swallowed with my love.

*

The Green Christ

A shamanic cure is based on an ancient teaching, a genetic knowledge about an unknowable will deep within our bodies that slowly grew into awareness along with the human race. We heard it in the music of our drums; we saw it in the light of our fires and we felt its strength in the power of our incantations. Shamen explored this perennial understanding of existance long before the Stone Age. We experimented and learned the terrifing truth about nature until eventually the overflowing of our wisdom became faith to the believer or philosophy in a more sceptical mind, but these speculations held no interest for us because they lacked the living experience of cosmogonic conciousness. Assuredly, shamen were, and always are, in reverent awe of the onnipotent will that hides behind the surfaces of reality. We have a sacred symbol to depict this driving energy. It is the foliate mask or Jack-in-the-Green: an image often found amongst the Gothic mythographs of medieval cathedrals. He usually appears as a smiling head formed from the leaves and branches of an architectural bush, although a more interesting instance is that of a man's horrified face with vines growing wildly from his screaming mouth (this is more acurate since fear is a human beings instinctive response to the numinous). Jack is our emerald Christ, or natures spirit, expessing itself though invicible signs and libidinal dreams. That is why a shamen ritualises. Our ceromonies are primoridial acts of worship to placate this relentless power; an attempt to channel potent forces away from the unhallowed gore acommpaning the irreligious negect of our duties. Yet external oblogations concell subconcious compulsions. To ignore the latter is only to detract from the former. So a robust David Beckham rejects the Green Knights severed head with his boot as it rolls towards him during the stylised battle of a football match. Or perhaps he may enlighten his darkness with a game of urban archary in the local pub after training. But on the pitch or at the bar civilised people living in their besieged suburban villages may sometimes still discover the meaning behind our antediluvian findings. Concider the Eucharist, where worshipers partake of a gods flesh and blood as spiritual food. Only the highly initiated are ready to taste him when he is taken down from the torture stake.

*

Drenched and dripping

With salted sweat

Our hands strangle

Each other's neck

In mutual love-making.

*

*

Damnation and desire
Reflect the black night of the numinous.

*

*

In a world of shadows the ideal may always become the Actual.

*

He has betrayed me.
Now I know the truth. At last I can guess his hidden schemes. Our relationship is already a thing of the past. Matthew has gone. The man who was an object of anxious desires to my best friend, while other men tried to fight for him in vain. A bastard that uneasy memories call up at sunset without ever revealing their treacherous origin and to which our temporary companions attributed in the imagination a wild lifestyle both perverse and attractive. Call him cunt, tease, or vampire and why not? He is the final manifestation of all my amorous anger. A sorcerer, manipulating subconscious sexual fears.

Endarkened by his sudden departure I can understand the nature of Matthew's influence. Freud almost guessed it and in the last decade I have heard skilled therapists discuss these overwhelming forces like careless adolescents, wilfully oblivious to the emotional destruction they were about to unleash. Man's kingdom is to fall before the rising power of an ignorant promiscuity itself controlled by dangerous spirits. Darkness is gathering. Evil is about to be reborn from the rushing chaos of modern introspection.

Listen.

He has gone, but I can still hear him screaming incantations in my dreams. Matthew has gone. He has left me and I am afraid.

*

There is as much truth in joy as there is in pain.

*

Instances of Initiation

Homosexuals are shamen. It is not our fault or failure, because we are what God has made us. So if straight society needs to attribute blame for its inability to understand us, let them condemn their false deity or nature herself. Suffering and desire have awoken our souls. They are moments of intense personal insight. Perhaps this is why a deeply felt sense of awe is the most significant experience for a modern shaman. Indeed, it is astonishment felt to the point of transcendence that stimulates our essences into a more abstract and sophisticated relationship with the environment. Instances when the history of mankind or the moral reactions of a stranger almost seem to initiate individual consciousness into a more unified mentation. A shaman always becomes such as the result of an inherited perplexity.

So what distinguishes a true shaman from a simple humanist is that this amazement comes to the former from the world itself, whereas to the latter, merely from questioning traditional values. However, most human beings experience this sensation of wonderment no more than fleetingly, an unfortunate fact which effectively isolates nearly all shamen from their fellows. One could say that the more insensitive a man or a woman becomes, the less frightening and mysterious existence is for them. On the contrary, everything seems a matter of course. But in fact, the attribute at issue is not only one of intuition. There are plenty of intelligent people who lack this miraculous outlook. Many, if not most of them, are professionals: academics; lawyers; doctors; clergymen and the rest. Now, insofar as they are intelligent, and many of them undoubtedly are, they have little qualitative awareness. To such as these the world is like their sexual relationships: undemanding and anxious. They are neither fully conscious nor self aware within them. Such people are, for that reason, incapable of apprehending the world as illusive, still less enigmatic, except possibly in rare moments. Otherwise they restrict what limited sense of awe they have into an hour every weekend. Therefore, it may not seem a shocking or even a divine task to demand from the dispossessed and the downtrodden enough strength to reject conventional wisdom. In one sense there is no choice: either we all embrace the liberating power of Jean Jacques Rousseau's spiritual example or we lose our protection against the anger of an injured Earth. Yes, our religious expectations must raise themselves to a practical level whereby everyone's basic needs have been satisfied and we can all search for the sustenance of personal dignity. Then, each of our lives will prove why profane morality has failed to deliver us into the promised land of cultural perfection. Shamanism alone testifies that there is no salvific requirement for poverty, since the actual heaven of hot food in the real hell of damp, makeshift shelter bleeds a man dry to the bone.

*

Judged
By every moment
I did not love
My heart
Awaits eternity.

*

*

To possess
A gentle nature
Seems
To be a lost art.

*

*

Imagine my love

To experience each day

The same futility

In awakening to a world

Grown old with broken promises.

*

Black instincts

Boil

In the liquid hate

Of failure.

*

The venom of intellect
Is rivalled only
By the bile of hope

*

*

A sweet and deadly melancholy
Attracts my bewieldered soul
Into a haunted sea of homocidal dreams
Where forgotten yesterdays strangle tomorrows hope
And desperation poisons a saddened heart.

*

*

Conformity
Is best admired
From an insecure distance.

*

*

I pay
For my freedom
With poverty.

*

*

History is a conspiracy
Of mediocre minds.

*

*

Our poverty has made us strangers.

*

Disfigured Angels

In my teenage years there was Hermaphroditas and my heart was Hermaphroditas and I was my heart.

He was our life and our life was the light of my world.

A world made brilliant by an enlightening affection without which there was but darkness. Yet even this darkness glittered in our light and the darkness did not understand.

Nor did I understand with the seasons an unrequited friendship.

It seemed that we were young with youth and thought our affection would guide us to a perfect freedom. But all these things were in my teenage years and now grow dull with lost memories.

Inspiration alone remains.

*

My love

Holds the seed

Of unborn Saints

In snowdrops

Hidden by nocturnal bliss

From sentient

Deformity.

*

*

God created families

To torment the unsuspecting

And persecute the unwary.

*

*

There is a strange putrescence to life

Which

Somehow

Makes it more liveable.

*

*

The acrid smell of respectabililty

Reeks with the stale breath

Of a plastic Saviour...

Let the paralysed listen to the dead

And the living join strong hands

With life.

*

Carl Orff's Disciple

I am the inspired disciple of Orffian will. A dwarf minister obsessed with divine misery and the sacred need to atone. Wearing only a grey robe bearing the sacrosanct silver cross, I magically scream at the living-dead to awaken. Behold! My poetic powers have uncovered the black flame of self and revealed secret paths to a dark enlightenment. So, at last, we can see our lives as bright stars in the infinite night of the numinous. An ebony twilight in which gigantic horns are sometimes almost visible.

That is why a thousand planets rise and fall around my pulpit as I preach the eternal verities of Carl's music: living human blood, violence, and unadulterated beauty. Joseph Conrad sits with Marlon Brando in sanguine meditation amongst the shadows of my cubic cathedral. Damnation? All around us mountain ranges crumble, yet our faith in phenomenal evil is transfigured by a clairvoyant vision into nature's cruel heart. In the perpetual nightmare of our world, surrounded by predestined portents, there is no hope but there is happiness. We are either powerless victims or temperamental heroes in the blind and rushing chaos of universal history. Then let the oceans freeze, while above the ice nine deadly moons shine in a wintry sky so that Orff can compose the fiery music burning within his soul. Only art is salvific and music is the highest of the arts. Yet the aesthetic sense is not merely an expression of ignorant Cartesian man but a lyrical voice that sings in mystical songs. A cognitive call by wild and basic instincts to dull mammalian brains. Forget intelligence. Ignore reason. Our magic conducts a nocturnal symphony in which we reveal the significance of sexual values. So, chanting Venusian hymns, my solemn congregation starts to throw yarrow leaves as a prayer to the dawning sun. After all, their tactile desires are assured everlasting success if they embrace the sensorium with a careless bliss. Listen ! Bataille's voice has become an angry angelus choiring the responsorial groan of a divinised humanity. A melody where each note is like the precious sweat which jewels his glistening head with a triumphant crown. Yes, our church elders enjoy the turbulent harmonies that resound throughout human heredity.

Therefore, as the friends of Carl Orff we need to use our religious will to transform animal emotions into an eloquent rhapsody of personal excess. In which case a free imagination is the magical aim my adepts seek to achieve. An immortal and creative spirit that finds individual meaning in this otherwise Dionysian world.

*

Am I bitter
About a low birth
Pre-ordained by Setibos
For the freedom
Of my soul?

*

*

Our English grimoire is the book
Of human nature itself. Within its hallowed
Text I can read spiritual depths
Hidden to the profane eye.

*

Noble Savagery

Man ritualises. That is what Crowley should have said. Each human essence is defined by sex and spirituality which form the age-old rites of personal significance. For example, every night we all spin the star-tongued sorcery that gets a partner into bed for a good shagging and then estimate our individual worth upon the performance. We rise in the morning with the sun, we eat, we drink and finally we go to work in the eternal regularity of life. Indeed, even science needs endless repetition in its attempt to grasp reality. This is why the theory of ritual behaviour could be called magic as daily we explore the foundations of rationality into the mystery of consciousness through our hopes and dreams. Only cyclic obsessions hold the key to human perfection. So if magic is the knowledge of the struggling social outcast, then I embrace it as my own.

Now as it has been my fate to enjoy excessive mystical experiences and, having the good fortune to belong to a homosexual coven, the wonder of which still evokes fear and turmoil in my mind, I have decided to write a psycho-sexual confession in order to describe my journey into an esoteric world. No-one, since the days of Casanova or Don Juan has ventured upon such an exhausting spiritual path until these modern times. Therefore, I have allowed myself no illusions as to the problems involved in trying to outline the activities of a modern pagan. They are very great and not only subjective, although these would be profound enough but, alas, my difficulties are of a more direct variety. This is because I no longer own any objective proof that my pilgrimage actually took place. The photographs, diaries and passports documenting the geographical aspect of my journey have been misplaced in the years of confusion which have elapsed since then, along with many of my memories. Poverty and unemployment have more than taken their toll. Nowadays, my recollection as well as my confidence have been considerably weakened. Lastly, I should also mention that I am handicapped by an oath never to speak about my occult work, even though I am permitted freely to discuss arcane ideas and symbols, provided that our bund itself is never openly explained. Also, despite the fact that the circle appears to be broken, no threat or entreaty would extract from me the answers to certain questions. On the contrary, if today the police gave me the option of a good kicking or divulging the secret of our sect, I would accept the agony of a violent beating.

Yet the philosophy of pleasure is a difficult faith to follow in Brixton. An area where terminal inertia conspires with futility to frustrate every known aspiration. Only drugs relieve the pressure. Only cheap lager dulls the pain. Without the basic vices of gambling and gluttony life would be intolerable. So I have learned to laugh at the lofty words of high and mighty men who lecture the poor on poverty from positions of financial strength. They come here all the time with educated ambitions, while remaining professionally blind to the problems of an impoverished borough. No-one wants real change, just the hyperbole of progress.

Well then, fuck the monarchy.
Fuck Parliament.
Fuck all the universities and every intolerant church.
The cadaverous hands of their dying authority are still trying to strangle my revolutionary revels, but the soul of virtue will triumph over them. After all, I am the fighting monk of universalism. A pagan preacher screaming ecstatic sermons that will not be silenced by the stupid or the weak. Therefore, listen to me. Everybody listen to me and be saved by the unholy truth. The facts tell us that mankind is a sub-species of Simeon, living on the crusty surface of a molten ball in the middle of nowhere. They say that no god can redeem us and that no Messiah or king can protect us from ourselves. All we have in the whole universe is each other. In which case the only choice a man can ever make is to cower like a fearful animal or to become a magical child who will conquer time and identity with immortal life. However, in practice, nearly everybody decides to remain a shivering monkey since most people are afraid of their freedom.

That is why it may seem a shocking or even a divine task to demand from the dispossessed and the vulgar the necessary strength to reject conventional wisdom. But I have no choice. Either we embrace the liberating power of perversion or we perish. Yes, our political expectations must raise themselves to a sensual level whereby everyone's basic needs have been satisfied and we can all search for the sustenance of personal dignity. Then fuck secular society too. There is no salvific value in poverty since the actual heaven of hot sex in the real hell of a damp bedsit drains a man dry to the marrow.

It is because profane morality failed to deliver us into the promised land of cultural perfection that sometimes have said Crowley developed a highly sophisticated form of magical humanism: his attempt as a British free-thinker to solve apparently perennial ethical problems. Well, it is certainly true, and I think this is an abiding characteristic of his work, that he thought love was so powerful it needed all the force of an awakened will to protect humanity from its uncontrolled bliss, although a life seriously devoted to tantric union with eternity was far from easy to live as it had intoxicating sexual demands. Nevertheless, Crowley saw our titanic fight against individual limitation as vital to human emancipation. Thus his ferocious intellect was stained with the mud and urine of absolute truth. A stance only true initiates could stomach.

It can be noted here that since the last international journal of Literary Criticism was published detailing Crowley's naturalist notes, several books on sexology have appeared on the market in which their authors (one suspects only in part subconsciously) have given the misleading impression that they were linked with our coven. Some of them have even suggested that they remain indebted to us for the sensual explorations that accompanied our journey into subtle spheres. Incidentally, even the preposterous claims of John Holmes come under justifiable suspicion from unbiased commentators. But they have nothing to do with us or our expeditious work, any more than the born-again bigots of small, sanctimonious assemblies have to do with the moral order by which they legitimise their repressed lives. Let me also say that, even if Austin Spare traversed the atavistic states he discusses, and if Phillip Rawson really tasted the ecstasies of India, their journeys were pedestrian compared to ours, since they feared the forbidden fruit of anal intercourse, the one true method to achieving magical potency. Whereas we, at certain stages of our pilgrimage, although generally aided by commonplace transport such as railways, motorbikes and aeroplanes, actually flew like lovebirds to the sacred sabbat. An occasion where Hermaphroditas, the founder of our Order, begged the Goddess Virgo to allow the mutual rape of himself with the fairy Salmacis so that they could steal each other's sexual potency to become one flesh together.

But once again my mammalian mind has lost the mystery of that eternal hour when we understood how androgynous angels were born not made and stood petrified before the power within ourselves.

Perhaps there was a general readiness at this time to explore psychic conditions beyond the mechanistic paradigms of high street retail managers. Then again, it may be that actual tensions between the spirit world and right-wing accountants had reached an impossible pressure. Whatever the case, many brilliant experiments in integrative psychology took place even though very little was achieved in practise. Only a few barriers were overcome. An advance was made here, a breakthrough there. This may be why our odyssey was often seen as a pioneering mission into a futuristic psychiatry, or the dark dabblings of a forbidden witchcraft. Either way, myth and imagination became the tools of our nocturnal trade. Magical herbs and exotic drugs stimulated a feeling of beatification wherein we brutally murdered each other's false egoic bodies to become cells in a single cortex. A sacrifice where life blood, or spirit if one prefers, is exchanged on the deepest of symbolic levels.

Let me mention at this point that the homo-erotic heights to which our arrogant ambitions climbed were shameless in their potential divinity. They required a control of body and mind very rarely attained in modern western society. As such these experiences can only be made fully comprehensible to the reader if the essential characteristic of our coven is openly explained. There were quite definite orgiastic aims forming the Dionysian design of our group despite the fact that every communicant had his own personal goal: a goal which was in its turn woven into our overall destination. In an initiatory sense, without these private projects our whole journey would have lacked the necessary force of magical catharsis that we needed to reach animal or mineral awareness. Certainly my own goal was a complex one. Even Leonard, our Grand Master, questioned me for hours about my plans before he accepted me into the emerald circle. However, most members of our coven had set for themselves quite simple quests which at that time I felt had missed the mark offered by this truly arcane opportunity. Only a few of my brethren in any way rivalled the heroic madness that obsessed me. For example, one of them was a petty criminal who coveted the sultry delights of a hidden Sufi monastery somewhere in the Takla Makan desert. Still another, an Oxford academic of renown, was attempting to experiment with alchemical slag: a substance that he stressed was vital to our fortunes, although in practice he was much more interested in profane rather than philosophical gold. Yet with hindsight my own objectives were ambiguous. The fundamental desire which had driven me since adolescence was to wrestle naked with Green Jack, the ancient spirit of the woodlands. We would fight until we were both drenched in sweat and I could make him ejaculate into the cauldron of creation. Then I would drink the completed elixir while still thundering with orgones. An act of wiccan magic that promised to make me as immortal as the seasons.

*

Dark night
Of glittering virtue
Sweet wanderer
In the sacred waste
My Prospero
I love your mystery.

*

*

Every fibre
Of endarkened feeling
Is needed to achieve
True being
Before
Setibos.

*

*

Light at last
Has darkly dawned
With hot sweat
And narcotic smoke
Still pleasently deluding
The dull dreams
Of an angry age
Awaiting
Judgements dawn.

*

*

Good and evil
Are merely different horns
Upon the head
Of Prospero.

*

*

Setibos
Grows green blosom
On my parents apple tree
To enjoy it whither
And die.

*

*

Flames of error
Burn my soul
From the arse of damnation
To torments day.

*

*

A single breath
Upon another
Allows our diseased flesh
To bear the unnatural tension
Of existence.

*

*

At last
Erotic aeons arise
Whose spiritual children
Will celebrate
The crowning success
Of sorcerous conquerors.

*

Our Sweetgrass Supper

Above Faram
far above the penumbra of a previous predition
I tripped to the beattitude of a better beat
along a lane of cold harbours
(where even magic is possible)
discoving the distant filth of an infinitesimal glory

Petros Koukoulomatis walked beside me, friend, soulmate,
we shared the disease of differentiation,
excluded by the bleak magnificance that mantles poetic genes
and marks a man with the damnable sign of a forbiden
beastiality.
We were arguing as snarled our way to a drunken truce in the
"phunky monkey",
"Look at that bottle" he said, "it is a palace of exaggerations
holding the blood of a god in it's belly
an alcoholic ocean of deppresed depressents seeking
expression
through dance and delirium".

Despite what you say there are three divine themes.

    Wine =   the dark substance of divinity.
                   Unknowable and unknown,
                   our intoxication expresses the
                   essence of unadulterated joy.

    Smoke = Earth's daughter and our true
                   pleasure. To be fully human is
                   to embody the vaporous mysteries
                   of time and torment that relentlessly

transform this material world.

Flesh = the active tissue of everyone's
sensual will. Its power is to inform
our appreciation of life as the
presence of paradise amongst us.

I screamed in anger and sung a heretics song in response,

Archetypal angel
who guards the gate of heaven
holy is your hidden name
let the new aeon come
and the higher law be done
in star-bright paradise
as it is on earth
give us ambrosia each day in joy
since we refuse restrictions fire
forgetful of our weaknesses
deliver us all to truest will.

*

Shakespeare's Dilemma

In his epilogue to The Tempest, Shakespeare begs his audience through Prospero's mouth to set him free from the enchanted island of theatre. He tells us that, as a poet, his own strength is faint and that he is imprisoned until our applause releases him back to his earthly life. But this asks the unthinkable. Prospero is much more interesting as a Renaissance magus than as the Duke of Milan, just as Shakespeare the Bard has an existence that exalts the career of a mere English author. Therefore we will never let him leave the land of sorcery or the stage of genius.

a

a

Repetition develops the worth of a word
Repetition evolves a sense of semantics
Repetition constructs every type of a text
Repetition reveals the meaning of meaning
Repetition unlocks each inclination of language

aaa

a

a

a

aa

a

*

Mistakes the size of tears
Well up within my clouded eyes
Until, like Caliban
The weakness of yesteryears
Makes me cry again.

*

One Substance Mind

Nature	God	Heaven	Value
Society	Soul	Culture	Interiority
Person	Body	Feeling	Instinct

Then

Spirit = Life = Consciousness = Individuation = Life

So higher consciousness = immortal life

Because Nature = Mind

An absolute substance of living matter

True Pantheism

which embodies transcendental values

like a human idea

whose only God is nature.

Theseus and the Minotaur

Masculinity thrives on competition. It has its own mysticism in the shared and sensual desire to physically strive with another man. Therefore as an act of living magic the art of wrestling is a sacred meditation. A possibility both spiritual and actual. Opponents burn with the unfathomable need to overcome each other's strengths. They hope to fully taste the limits of their capacities as men in a formidable act of will. Indeed, from the Golden Age of Greece down until today, creative violence has been acknowledged as the essential key to establish a deep feeling of holy fraternity with the titans. A step into the magical ring of Olympian combat as equal heroes in an ageless drama enables a man to fight ecstatic battles into imaginations height, thereby achieving a peak of muscular pleasure. Powerful young bodies stretch and strain against each other drenched in the sweat produced by agony and bliss. In a deadly dance of gnostic truth a secret language is spoken directly between two hot bodies afire with pain.

Yet, my first consciously magical battle was only a tentative ritual, although it contained the certainty that I must embrace a warriors path, even as a poet. After all, everything is a question of appropriate attitudes. A sudden urge, a few taunts and, like the Minotaur, my fate was changed forever. I knew that the profane could never take a leap into the unknown of this labyrinth. Thesis and antithesis locked in the synthesis of struggle. Agile fingers interlocked, grunting like two bears we came together in the form of a living pentacle. Pleasure, sensuality, excitement, all intensified to a tremendous pitch. Our legs entwined, I felt the almost electrical experience of awareness itself. Purity alone understands when this intimacy is exchanged. Breathing heavily, chest firmly against chest, we gradually exerted greater and greater force until some furious wrestling was under way. During the course of our match I bridged my back to slow down my enemy. NO! I felt that I was losing. NO! Then Theseus snarled like an animal and growled out the word "YES". He sat on my stomach with his will beating down upon me like a blow.

We both collapsed at that moment. Panting. Tired.

With passionate ambition and explosive aim, Theseus had spoken a private vow which called in a primordial voice to the forests and the hills of an ancient world. Whereas in myself I felt new powers. I enjoyed new strengths. So without pulling back one inch, Theseus and I achieved a new relationship closer than any mere blood tie.

Suggestions for the ordinand to perfect this simple but nevertheless powerful act-

Read the myths.
Sculpt the body into an engine of righteous will.
Become healthy. Feel strong. Let the powers of
Heaven and Earth build up to a point of necessary ritual.
Perfume the body with pine.
Intoxicate the mind with virtue.
Arrange a feast of skilfully spiced speeches.
Recline on warm blankets exhausted and magically
Transformed by practical art.

Name and Form

My nickname at school revealed a spiritual truth. From the inherited name of PARRY an occult transliteration took place, as I became physically stronger I was rebaptised with the incomprehensible title of PARRAZENO. Shortly afterwards this too changed and my true name became ZENO, the philosopher who didn't believe in motion. Prophetically I knew even then my classmates had unconsciously named my primordial shape. The Pagan dwarf ZEN - O, a master of oriental poetry.

>Fallow fields
>Devoid of life and blight
>Need the incessant prayer
>Of sexuality
>As their salvation.

*

*

Far beneath

The atomic passions

Burning

Our youthful star

My skin bubbles

And blisters

In a silent spell

Of unknown terror

To Setibos

Who above

The most distant sphere

Sits in stern judgement

Upon innocence.

*

*

Your ebony hair
wild as youth
smells of pleasure.

Your charcoal eyes
deep as passion
glaze with desire.

Your Grecian nose
perfect as marble
warms to ardour.

Your rosebud mouth
sweet as yesterday
moans in ecstasy.

Your slender cheeks
taut as hunger
blush at delight.

Your sturdy chin
firm as character
arouses my rapture.

Your angelic face
strong as beauty
entices and excites.

*

> Desire is the greatest virtue
> Because "I will" hides beneath each prayer
> As the evolutionary struggle towards
> Identity is slowly interiorised.

*

There is very little that I can say with confidence about Darren, as his sapphire eyes betrayed a maturity which his flesh denied. Sometimes he would speak to me in dreams, and I rarely saw him physically. On those mysterious occasions he used to meet me at a time and place meticulously fixed in advance. We would drink German beer, discuss certain trends in contemporary literature, and the philosophy of Arthur Schopenhauer.

For myself, I believe that he is a human being living on this earth but possessed of terrible powers. Although, by this, I do not mean that when we met I experienced the feeling of intense physical depression that accompanies a loss of personal orientation. On the contrary, I felt that I was in the presence of a force so powerful that I can only compare it to the shock one would receive from being too near a falling thunderbolt. This was followed by nervous prostration and I experienced at the same time great difficulty in breathing, along with a sharp ringing in the ears.

Yet he was so fearsome. A man could only admire him and be shaken.

*

*

Tomorrow

Priests and Poets

Will serve

The word of love

As ithyphallic bards

Inspired by Setibos.

*

*

Poetry is a question

Of calligraphic consciousness

And words.

*

Recridescent Laments

Before the beginning was silence. Dark and perfect. Immaculate. An infinite void without any pretensions.

In the beginning was the song. Light and creation. Sentience. A finite actuality of culture, meaning, value and the sacred possibility of thought.

After the beginning will be silence. Tragic and profound. Beauty. All action lost in the momentary past of a single chant.

I am the word. My true name is Poetry. Everything is made through my work as an author. Language creates order out of a primal incoherence. Gardens of experience grow because of their occult properties. Indeed, our very souls are made of metaphors which may place a man on the moon or explore the full eternity of flesh. Therefore, language is clearly Divine.

And yet my story seems to live in the face of silence.

*

My bedroom smells of Jasmine flowers and semen.

*

I understand love.

Ferdinand was my centre. The principle need of my otherwise estranged soul. A friend transfigured by type and talent into a mirror of myself. An ancient heart I rediscovered by our accidental predestination.

But sometimes, when we feel like fighting, it is still possible to believe that there are young men above him in my affections whose athletic beauty is far greater than his, as his intellect is superior to that of the naturally gifted. Indeed, there is no reason why there should not be higher men altogether beyond my eternal attraction to Ferdinand. Yet in reality I already know this is untrue as his friendship inspires me with a magical vision. It makes me suspect that there exists a certain point of consciousness where love and anger, flesh and blood, even the past and future cease to be conceived as separate; becoming each other in the freedom of spontaneous experience.

One would search in vain for a union closer than this.

*

> We ate each other's anger
> On the altar of anxiety.

*

The failure of mainstream Christianity to address contemporary views of sex and sorrow has left a moral vacuum within our society. A speciel void where the search for personal meaning and value is attacked by blind convention on one side and a superficial commercialism on the other. Fearfully, the whole notion that an inherited ethic is somehow superior to the living morality found through self-examination and prayer remains as insincere now as it was in the time of Jesus Christ. Modern Pharisees may pay lip service to the idea of family values and basic social homogeneity but they are no less spiritually insidious than their ancient counterparts.

*

A Gnostic Ministry

. My rule is to train in the higher law of the Soul.
. My rule is to train in the tactile mysteries of sexual delight.
. My rule is to train in the use of exotic drugs and holy liqueurs.
. My rule is to train in the creative ethics of unashamed selfhood.
. My rule is to train in the magical labour appropriate to everlasting success.
. My rule is to train in the mutual service existing amongst the wise.

*

*

I preach mutation as a spiritual practice.

*

*

Love is surely

The most pleasant

Of all metaphysical diseases.

*

Nietzsche's Donkey

At the centre of Zarathustra's moral musing lies his rejection of Israel's beast. An ignorant Jewish donkey braying ethical platitudes in the silent midnight of perpetual chaos. Beware! Their god is an unclean Egyptian devil poisoning our innocent European hearts with the materialistic bile vomited up by Hebrew financiers. Why else would a stupid ass rejoice in a perverse festival with so called higher men? Surely, Nietzsche's alter ego felt sick to his Iranian stomach.

This parody of an animal arrogantly claims a forbidden sovereignty over Caucasian thought. Obscene! Zarathustra's mistake was to divide Aryan moral experience into two opposing categories. The former and most important "Good", allegedly possessed an archetypal necessity, whereas the latter "Evil", was contingent and therefore demonic. So this last class, deprived of all permanent significance, was judged to be somehow inferior because the virtue of stability was seen as redeeming in an insecure world such as our own. Nowadays it would take a Superman, untainted by

Zarathustra's original error to live a strong and spontaneous life.

Yes, Zarathustra must return to cure the world of its degenerate consciousness.

However, under the pressure of need, our irregular views have revealed the dynamic flow hidden within sacred history. Apuleius was temporarily blinded when he hinted at golden mysteries glittering inside a mule's head. Also, Zacharius was struck dumb when he realised that his perennial philosophy did not originate in the burning eyes of a brazen beast. Indeed, donkey-headed demons have always haunted the Jewish mind with an uneasy nostalgia. Thus we find in the Gospels that Christ rode on the back of a donkey as a clear declaration of his royal divinity to a rebellious Sanhedrin. An open act of theological warfare against established animality. The totem, for some, had become taboo.

Yet on closer inspection the religious superiority of this Jewish teacher is sacrosanct precisely because he reacted against dead authority. Furthermore, his preaching stressed the value of intentional suffering as a means towards salvation. That is, of an evolutionary struggle for personal emancipation. As a result, the moral stagnation of Hebraic man was shown to be an unsteady balance tipped towards the formation of a specific task. The preservation of a communitarian attitude at the expense of individual liberty. In which case his battle against the beast of mindless autocracy was as remarkable as it was vital for the progress of social and psychological advancement. He was guilty of blasphemy against the herd. He stood as a libertarian for the unfettered individual. His insurrection inevitably weakened the spiritual claims of modern Judaism by proclaiming that every man was a king and a demigod.

We need to fight for our freedom. If Nietzsche had been more heroic he would have observed that it cannot arise naturally. Neither can it be given. Zarathustra will return to Europe, as the final conflict must be here. Our higher law has always needed German culture to inflame the spark of Aryan wisdom into a raging fire whereby all are warmed and enlightened.

*

The name "I will" is a religious goal
A new testament which transformed our
Western minds by fermenting a
Selfish wine in theological bottles.

*

I ache

To see your naked body

Draped in the white sheets

of Midnight's dark.

*

Butterflies

Halo the bowels

Of my beloved

With rainbows

At noon.

*

*

A Homosexual must be willing
To live
And breathe
Deformity
In order to create
Or reveal
Beauty.

*

*

With blood and might
I'll bring to being
A dark insight.

*

Sorcery

Ideas are light within the brain: entoptic relationships. The interaction of the phenomenal world with the noumenon. So intuition can therefore be seen as a pathway into evermore refined states of mentation. By light we transform spirit into nature. Indeed, these shapes find their counterparts in the esoteric designs of Witchcraft. Non-representational diagrams that evoke supersensual powers. Their basic elements are the point, the line, circle, square, triangle and the pentagram symbol. In different combinations they express certain primary configurations which condition the manifestation of the horned god. They also form the scaffold upon which a higher immortal body is built.

The meaning of these shapes is vital to witches, which is why I sat on my bed day and night, turning the Philosopher's stone over and over in my mind. I explored every detail until I reached an instinctive conclusion which I then tested against the abstract speculations of the alchemists. But the dilemma of unverifiable subjective interpretation always arose: a problem which I learned can only be overcome by increased analysis and comparative insights into the nature of mind itself. However, I slowly began to realise that inner light is related to the implementation of purpose because spirits are like numbers. My essence seemed to live in a numerical field in which individual geometric figures appeared as energic phenomena. So every number became its own pattern of spiritual relationships that may materialise in a myriad of forms, whether in chemical combinations or primitive human interactions.

*

Our liberated lives
Lead us to search
Like the crawling Scarabaeus
For magical meaning
Within the glittering darkness
Of perpetual night.

*

*

At last
Phallic aeons arise
Whose erotic children
Will achieve
The liberating success
Of infernal conquerors.

*

Moon-calves

In my opinion most professional religionists are, as such, worldlings in a pejorative sense. It is important to remember that throughout history priests have pandered to the superstitions of the people, and their "careers" often involved ingratiating themselves with rich patrons. Furthermore, up to the present day, spiritual authority is still given to an intellectually redundant Church which tries to claim a legitimacy over our natural sense of awe. This is why the greatest magical humanists from Edward Lord Herbert to Aleister Crowley have perpetuated a campaign against official Christianity. After all, these religious authoritarians were then, as are most of them now, led to spirituality not by a sense of bliss but by a feeling of power. Their first encounter with the idea of transcendence is as members of an ideologically active organisation and through the doctrines of renowned authors, which they may or may not understand, depending upon their experiences. Some of them go on to defend and expound these cerebrations. If they then distinguish themselves at this, organised religion offers them the opportunity of making a respectable living. Therefore subservience rapidly becomes the means by which they are provided with employment. It becomes one way amongst others of surviving in society and in a hostile world. But all of this is in reaction to external, not internal, stimuli.

*

There is a Hell
Prepared for those
Who refuse to love.

*

Only very old friends make such bitter enemies.

*

Transfigured Wrestlers

I once fought with a young actor for the love of a very good friend. He stood at the end of his lounge completely naked and almost exactly as Colin de Plancey had described him. The tempter had a strong chest, powerful arms and stood just over six feet tall. Indeed, Alex was perfectly proportioned with refined sensual features. A strikingly handsome Persian. Impatiently he began to walk towards me to wrestle it out. As he did, I quickly unbuttoned my clothes until I stood equally naked and faced him. We both looked at each other for a moment in silent satisfaction.

Then he stretched out his arms as if to embrace me and I stepped forward to meet his grasp. He bore down upon me. I met with him fiercely. In that Olympian instant we fell together, locked and quite inseparable, upon the soft carpeting. Physical arrogance made our fight heroic. Alex tried to hold me down by twisting around and lying on my back while using his legs to bind me. However, he was unable to gain the upper hand, so he tried to weaken me by using his body to crash down, again and again, on top of my shoulder. But I caught hold of his neck and pulled him to the floor. We rolled over each other to the corner of the room. Suddenly he bit my chest. I howled with pain and instinctively slapped him heavily in the stomach. He released his hold. At last, pressing my unexpected advantage, I caught his neck in a stranglehold with my arm and he held my throat tightly with his hands. By this time we were both dripping wet with sweat, although neither of us wanted to give up. Alex and I were born fighters, so we continued to wrestle for hours in the twilight of a miraculous evening, until our argument was solved at a deeper level. Alex the actor gradually became transfigured by fear and ferocity into a trusted companion.

*

Never fuel the unlikely with an improbability.

*

*

Love is for Poets

The unhappy children

Of a better world.

*

Raw Radiance.

God is as *Ren*, the secret name.
    Light illumines *Sekem*, our energy and power.
        Flame fans *Khu*, my guardian angel.
        Therefore
Behold the colour of *Ba* - my heart
    and
      enjoy the illusions of a double *Ka*
        Yet fear Hades
        as it hides
        in the shadows
        of *Khaibit*
While rejecting *Sekhu* as a material corpse
      since our minds
      are unified
        in the Spirit
      With light as the key
               to their enlightenment

As Saint Paul said in Corinthian Vision
                because
                    the circulation of a risen Christ is
                    a golden rose
                    in the Kingdom's
        everlasting sight
So speak to a pure spark in the Persian poet Rumi and learn
                    from his burning body
to find communion with hidden Cherubs who imitate Jesus
by being reborn
like flares of fire in an Egyptian desert
or as
the light of the world
in a Nazarene night
              with a glittering eye
              inside an unmanifest God
whose Logos
        is an Aristotelian brilliance
                    born itself from brilliance
on Pentecostal Sundays
        afire with truth
        my
        Father
        Ren
    Holy Spirit   Son
      Khu   *Sekem*
        dwells
inside a bush ablaze with life
        Our Saviour
        who will be what he will be

                    as heat
            renewing the whole of nature
with singing Seraphs standing above a dazzling Chakra Circle
                spinning solitude
            upon the loom of experience
            in which
            Elijah
            promised Elisha
                a second portion of his Soul
to save him from becoming
                a shade
            without a solid aura
                    or a crystallised salvation
in delusion land
which never sees
the black light of magical glory
        or the sorcerous art
                    in a dark Dante's modern insight
                    into the profound desires
                    of a triple illumination
                    along our radiant path
                    to Absolute Being

                            *

Incantations

As I chant, my soul seems to realise that the world is my other self as well as the path of the eternal. Every perfumed breeze on an autumnal evening is really my own breath. Amber leaves shiver only when I sigh. Then as I walk to a nearby stream, the water that I take to drink is my blood. It refreshes me with its purity and strength. The good Earth that I feel beneath me is as much my body as are the muscles and sinews that I use to express my inviolable purpose. Even the fire that my friends sit around is actually the warmth of my spirit. The immortal flame of life itself.

*

My priestly robe symbolises
A single-minded dedication
To the mysteries of matter.

*

Via Negativa

Our qualified Chaos is a crazed eight-winged God whose only son is Reason. He tries to structure the nightmares that his Father dreams into different spheres of nature but, just like a madman, the Lord's mind keeps changing its shape in the perpetual motion of divine thought. Therefore, Reason lives a life of despair.

*

As a Pagan I believe in the past mastery of Christ,
The relentless inhumanity of God
And the necessity of true will.

*

The Fool and His Fathers

*

        Dionysus speaks through me like intelligent light.

I saw the spirits of a material selfhood agonise under an oppressive fixation,
examining endlessly intoxicating entheogens within apocalyptic tenements...
patrolled by the blackest angels.

I have danced in the darkness that transfigured the earth as it gleamed supernal,
my flat nose anointed by the ever-living poppy oils which sacralised my dwarfish body beautiful,
itself adorned by a threadbare cassock.

I fought with leather demons breathing flaming rectal fumes,
while niched golden-heads paraded around a public explanation,
hoping satellite dust would settle upon their secular sacrifices.

        Dionysus speaks through me like intelligent light.

*

*

On my own

Lonely way home

In the morning's golden day

I can still feel

The scented touch

Of your strong young body

Pressed firmly against me.

*

*

Pride enters sin
Like poison
In the wound
Of a soul.

*

Montparnasse

Before going on to consider the problems raised by the idea of chaos I would like to put Baudrillard in the correct context. For me, Jean Baudrillard is, as it were, the frame of the picture. An inspired Parisian terrorist trying to force the human mind from its monistic superstitions and release it into the full plurality of truth. Baudrillard seems to believe that philosophical method, along with a misunderstood monotheism blinds our contingent eyes to an undefinable, unrepresentable and infinitely mysterious reality. To perceive does not mean that we know in the pure sense, as others may perceive differently. However, he thinks that an open and mystical science is the formula for advancing human spirituality. Yet we know how severely Baudrillard is opposed by those who resist liberation. Reasonable men and women (so called) who defend accepted logic or moral notions with an idolatrous zeal. Those who need to hide behind a method, or protect themselves as representatives of a discipline, instead of seizing new and higher values. Baudrillard's critics say that his tactics will lead to anarchy.

Good. The evolution of ideas has never relied upon a rationalist caution but on a sorcerous elite with the superior intelligence only an unfettered imagination can give. Wisdom for Baudrillard is found in the necessary confession that many stars light our intellectual path to higher consciousness. A realisation that Baudrillard himself proselytises in an enthusiastic defence of spiritual freedom.

*

*

Fallow fields

Devoid of life and blight

Need the incessant prayer

Of sexuality

As their salvation.

*

*

My primary school
Was not so much tedium
As Te Deum.

*

*

The leaning lintels of Durdle Door

Stood crystalled

Beside beclouded walls

Of innocent ice

As siren songs made their music

Within a frosted imagination

By silver stars.

*

Mysticism is not an attempt to escape the truth through sweetening the world with sugar and spice. At least it shouldn't be. Anyone in search of religions and therefore transcendental truths has a duty to see creation in all of its horror as well as its light in order to give a clear description of the spiritual realm. Anything less is a sacrifice of human intellect upon the altar of sentimentality. As John Bunyan said in his author's apology to the Pilgrim's Progress, 'some men by feigning words as dark as mine, make truth to spangle, and it's rays to shine'.

*

We shall not die

But meet again

As crimson clouds

Upon the brimstone winds

Of the desert

*

I have danced in the darkness which illumined the earth
As it gleamed beneath a hidden perfume.

*

*

I have surmounted my pain but not always my regrets.

*

*

Her silver horns ascended

Through a dusky sky

That sparkled with rapturous stars

Above azure seas washing forever ashore

Small golden grains of gentle sand

Upon this deserted country coast

In Southern Spain.

*

Henry Two Horn

And I beheld Rollins coming up out of a multi-media Earth: and he had two horns like a lamb and he spake like an executive. Yet there was neither a night or a day in the global economy in which he was to be heard, so he built a tower of babble along the superhighway and from thence intoned a muscular career. This is why there are lies and there are damned lies. Cubic lies. Sometimes whole cities are built with these lies and the painful darkness of human life is doubled within them. Thus great corporations of greed compete with expanding industrial estates in their efforts to dehumanise the world. Indeed, a channel of free and evil access televised Canary Wharf Tower as the body in which mammon himself would incarnate. One can see the luminous pyramid of his wicked brain flashing insidious messages over the country he came to rule. Be warned, his sterile red eyes forever sparkling above endless rows of shining teeth intend to observe your weaknesses and then devour your pleasures. That is why my intention is to follow a pagan precedent: I condemn Hollywood the whore to walk in darkness, and stumble in ignorance along an internet of human hells.

*

A single breath

Upon another

Allows our tortured flesh

To bear the unnatural weight

Of experience.

*

*

Victory is mine

In standing unloved

And alone

Before the cold angels

Of an indifferent heaven.

*

Spinoza's Lens

In order to achieve a right perspective I would like to take a brief look at that very modern figure Baruch Spinoza, and the spiritual hope which forms the cornerstone of his work. Now, I believe that in many ways the philosopher Spinoza's personal journey prefigures the trials as well as the opportunities promised by our allegedly post-modern age: an age which so often seems to claim that it has grown beyond the prophetic faith of Israel and the ethical teachings of Christianity. However, rather unlike this Saintly man, our society appears to be increasingly deluded instead of Enlightened. Allow me to expand upon this comparison: the philosopher Spinoza mirrors our present spiritual predicament because he was a Jew who unsuccessfully converted to Christianity, publicly disavowed the 613 precepts of the Torah and claimed that the state regulations of ancient Israel were applicable only to this theocracy which of course had long since vanished. Furthermore, Spinoza proclaimed that to truly worship God we must lead compassionate lives which embody justice and mercy to all human kind. Yet, in his own intolerant era, Spinoza had to disguise the Cabalistic roots of his philosophical outlook. Sadly, his own people did not want to hear him (and neither did the Church) precisely because of his non-dogmatic interpretation of the teachings of Judaism and he was subsequently expelled from the synagogue. This is one of the reasons why Spinoza changed his first name from the Hebrew, Baruch to the Latin, Benedictus. Now, Spinoza dismissed traditional conceptions of good and evil as well as notions such as pagan or Christian as he searched ever more deeply into the fundamental problems of human existence, asking supremely radical questions like, 'What is God ?'; 'What is a human being ?'; 'What would constitute Truth ?', and 'What is love ?'. Indeed, one of his greatest gifts was an ability to brush aside the merely conventional in favour of the indispensable. This may be due to the fact that his warm heart and brilliant mind was set on discovering the living Truth revealed within Sacred Scripture as he strived to find the 'Or Adonai', or the Light of the Lord. Moreover, through his fearless struggle with these ideas there arose certain majestic insights, which eventually became the very basis of his philosophical principles. He came to understand God as Creative Nature, the Ever-Being or Ens Perfectissimum which we can never conceive of as having been created or as having not existed. Our knowledge of God therefore as Essence and Substance, Spinoza believed, was the vital core of our own lives. In fact, it was the source of our identity. Thus, in a mystical sense, our minds are actually in God, or in other words our minds, as the Hebrew Sages of old expressed it, are Shekinah. That is, the indwelling of God. So, to the extent that a human soul envisions God or Creative Nature in Its Oneness and Eternity, the Elohenu and Echod of Toraic literature becomes Man himself, part of eternity, his ideas clear and adequate and his soul filled with intellectual love for God. Furthermore, this love, which was born out of philosophically educated prayer and meditation into the Divine order of the universe, (along with a complete acceptance or submission towards it's formations and modifications), naturally arouses compassion towards our fellows, since we slowly begin to realise that all is One. For Spinoza the love of God is identical with the love of man towards man. This intellectual love of God brings an awareness of Adonai, which in turn fills the human soul with a profound sense of gratification and beatitude. Moreover, when confronted by this great love human hatred and prejudice along with other confused or irrational perceptions rapidly disappear. In a sense, evil was ultimately a lie born from ignorance and confusion. Interestingly, Spinoza argued that disturbing passions are only the bodily manifestations of disturbing ideas: they are of the same order, or disorder, viewed in one instance as a form of the mind while again in another instance as a form of the body. Indeed, man himself was a form or modus in God: a sparkling drop in the vast surging ocean of causality.

*

Sweet moon

That shines with the twilight

Of premature death

And exposed bone

Learn to smile

Upon my lonely grave.

*

*

Because

The stain of ink

Covers my tired fingers

Many people will learn to dream

Of freedom.

*

*

Immortality wears orchids

Which resist

A puppet called death

And reclaim

The sarcedotal acres

Of a secret eden.

*

*

The grave alone shows mercy,

A paradise of everything

Regained.

*

*

As the dead who seek

To live a life immortal

We must remember

Beyond the beyond

And sing

In subtle states

A theophany of self-possession.

*

*

Dead minds

Enchain

Our fragile world

Of sensual thoughts.

*

*

I saw my gnosis
Take to the wing
Ascending from the world's desire
And choiring elementals
Around her sing the praise
Of change in sulpherous fire.

The tears of children
Shall wash her clean
While hellish loves her form enfold
Above material glories
She is seen
Surmounted on a throne of mould

Light and life
Are her sole aim
As witness to my skins decay
In whose embrace
She must remain
Until I die one lonely day...

I saw my Gnosis

*

*

I am pot

In which Setibos

Seeks to cook his thoughts.

*

Boatswain Thomas

Among the often neglected heroes of existentialist literature stands the enigmatic New Testament figure of the Apostle Thomas. He is a far more complex character than the Hebrew patriarch Job because Thomas is a man of faith who nevertheless refuses to believe in the resurrection of Jesus Christ until incontrovertible evidence is offered to him. Indeed, a strange momentum may be perceived in the Saint's sparkling vision which almost compels every pilgrim in search of the Absolute to deny both prophecy and dogma in order to embrace a life of perpetual self-examination. Our fractured and confusing world appears to provoke Thomas into regarding elaborate religious theories as a series of attempts to either mask, or wilfully reinterpret, the eternal verities even though an honest consideration of simple and obvious fact brought speculation back to spiritual truth. This is one of the reasons why this Apostle's radical rejection of religious hyperbole serves as a touchstone for all those Christian ethicists who are genuinely seeking an existential perspective. After all, Thomas objects to the initial confusion surrounding accounts of the resurrection not out of cynicism, but because these statements seem to him a travesty of the reverence due to Christ: a reverence which these accounts ironically claimed to affirm.

Thomas does not, of course, represent a positive ethical ideal. His life must surely have been tainted by this sense of 'Doubt' even when he was allowed to place his fingers in the side of the risen Christ. On one level this makes him the most fortunate man in history and certainly the only man in Holy Scripture to receive an evidential response from the Divine. Yet, on another level the character of Thomas anticipates the moral and spiritual conflict which in recent decades has baffled Christian scholarship and disturbed the status quo. As with Thomas, what started as a healthy and stubborn defiance of received wisdom became amongst the counter-culture the curse of a moral circularity which seems to have then steadily declined into a shallow and dangerous relativism. What is more, this disturbing trend has evoked notoriously inadequate opinions from Christian conservatives upon subjects as diverse as child pregnancies, urban delinquency, homosexuality and the necessary rejection of our society's professed rationality in their almost embarrassing efforts to hold back the forces of liberality. However, ones soul may be temporarily empowered through these manoeuvres but only because this process allows a dislocation to exist between ones inmost self and the world. It seems that Thomas has become emblematic for the contemporary Christian community and not the visionary Apostle John.

As a friend of Christ who is racked by scepticism and yet transfigured through authenticity, Thomas prefigures the Christian existentialists. One recalls pilgrims such as Berdyaev who prayed for collective meaning as well as priests like Haring who remind us that it is an individuals service that gives them a sense of value. Now, commentators of this calibre are vital for a better understanding of Thomas' position and curiously they reveal the somewhat tepid position adopted by those who have still to be inspired by his view: a stance which is quite unsatisfactory in two related ways. Firstly, it is unacceptable because it tries to deny the social implications of the existential and, secondly, by ignoring this spiritual thirst as the basis of the ethical life. However, if it is true that tensions between the ideal and the actual may be resolved in an authentic human being's public life, then it may also be the case that the agonising strain caused by this ethical timidity cannot delay the resolution of this tension for very long. Examples of this transformation which fascinate me and that are usually forgotten or 'theorised away' are found in the lives of men and women who spurn social triumphalism to lead a life of friendly devotion. In a way, these people form a hidden community bound together by the silent promise of virtue because, almost by accident, they embody the revolutionary spirit that eventually becomes a political initiative. Moreover, the ethical light which they shine upon society reveals a corruption as old as greed and a market-place where people are the economic fodder of multi-national companies without a conscience. Therefore, I suspect that Christian existentialism alone can perform the task which the Apostle Thomas would have recommended: the stimulation of friendly conduct as a medicine for post-modern ills.

*

His names overwhelm
The virtues of time
Whispered
By the gentle arabesque
Of demonic wings
That beat in obscene reverence
At pornopoetic dominion.

*

*

Trinculo awoke
In a forest of dead violets
To the scream
Of a woman
Or a world
As it seemed to him
The voice
Within every pain
That is known to man

*

*

I was born in Setibos
Grew in him
Lived at length
Laughed and cried
So that one day I shall even die
As flesh
To him
Who I love as one of my fathers.

*

*

Imagination is light
Within
A grey material brain.

*

*

Stood between the Noumenon
And his native soil
Prospero
Raised the raging sword
Of unrighteous fury.

*

Stephano

Just as the individual religious man has a divine mother in principle but only a fleshy father, so too the modern bi-sexual has for a father universal knowing and for a mother infinite love.

He feels her, although he can not behold her in his consciousness as an immediate object.

Therefore any reconciliation between these two aspects of awareness can only be found in the Noumenon.

Yet these radically different parents make quite opposite demands upon a person. Enlightened mind requires an isolated interiority, whereas the heart needs sensual justification in sexual union for love to fully flower towards both men and women.

Hence the historical dilemma in trying to discover an authentic spiritual path.

*

Trapped
In a desolate ghetto
Of defeating discussion
My only hope now
Is to make magic.

*

*

My memories of the enchanted island
Are
Like crystalline beads
Thread upon the golden string
Of
Identity.

*

*

The mindless years
Have run a post-modern journey
Into twilight reason
Where an unparalleled ignorance
Awaits all future reflection.

*

*

Hate is either
The phantom heart
Within a meaningless world
Or the slow emergence
Of an ultimate value.

*

*

Every fibre
Of endarkened feeling
Is needed to achieve
True being
Before
Setibos.

*

*

Is my life
To be seen
Amongst men
I
The very first
Of all fates eyes
In Milan.

*

*

We must cut
And slash
Our economic chains
With claws
Of stainless silicone
To imitate
Setibos

*

*

Like Sycorax
I oppose convention
And accept
The Homosexual truth
Of a higher law

*

oo

o

o

oo

o

o

oo

o

*

In the very ground of Being
I saw your sacred name
Setibos.

*

*

Through the evening
The people wail and moan
Until the sunset
When rose petaled liberation blooms.

*

*

Each moment reveals
The spiritual infinity
Contained
Within my tainted skin.

*

*

How can I study
Your magickal alphabets
And mystic symbols
When my heart
Is full of sadness?

*

*

I stirred Michael's mind
That barrel of tar
With my paper-spoon of reason
In the unfulfilled hope
Of discovering his humanity.

*

*

Ariel
Of white light
Your holy back
Has angels wings.

*

*

I am evil
Because the world
Is good.

*

*

I am both myth and man

Cannibal and Caliban.

*

Printed in the United Kingdom
by Lightning Source UK Ltd.
125869UK00001B/301/A